This book is for:

_____

The Very Best Teacher in the World

according to me:

_____

To all the amazing teachers, including my own: Mrs. Kimball,
Miss Anthony, Miss Stamm, Mrs. Bennett, Ms. Benson,
Mrs. Kaminer, Mrs. Rabinowitz, and Mrs. Horowitz—DJS

To Mrs. McEwan, Miss Melia, and all my other amazing teachers for their
patience and encouragement during my school years!—RH

GROSSET & DUNLAP
An imprint of Penguin Random House LLC, New York

First published in the United States of America by Grosset & Dunlap,
an imprint of Penguin Random House LLC, New York, 2022

Text copyright © 2022 by D. J. Steinberg
Illustrations copyright © 2022 by Ruth Hammond

GROSSET & DUNLAP is a registered trademark of Penguin Random House LLC.

Visit us online at penguinrandomhouse.com.

Library of Congress Cataloging-in-Publication Data is available.

Manufactured in China

ISBN 9780593386033   10 9 8 7 6 5 4 3 2 1 HH

MY TEACHER IS THE BEST!

BY
D. J. STEINBERG

ILLUSTRATED BY
RUTH HAMMOND

GROSSET & DUNLAP

The Welcome Tree

My teacher decorated our classroom wall
with leaves cut out in the colors of fall,
and on every leaf, take a look and you'll see,
there is somebody's name . . .
and this one says *me!*

Ms. Brainiac!

My teacher's got the biggest brain,
and I can prove it's so—
no matter what you ask her,
there's nothing that she doesn't know.

Book Magician

Whenever I want to find a book,
my teacher says, "Let's see . . ."
Then—*abracadabra*—she goes and picks
the perfect book for me!

Who *Is* That?

That can't be my teacher—
she *never* leaves school,
so it must be her double I see.
But then why is that lady
in a sweatshirt and jeans
smiling and waving at me?

Sick Day

I missed school today 'cause my nose
   caught a cold,
and my head got a little too hot.
Do you think my teacher missed me today?
'Cause I sure missed my teacher a lot!

A Mile-Wide Smile

My teacher has the best smile in the world,
and whenever one comes my way,
that mile-wide smile makes me feel
a mile tall the whole day.

World's Best Explainer

Whenever I'm confused,
confounded, or befuddled,
when my brain is getting tangled
and my mind is getting muddled,
my teacher comes right over
to give me a helping hand
and soon as he explains it all—
ta-da!—I understand!

Biggest Valentine

I used all the pink and red markers in Art
to make my teacher a ginormous heart.
And I added a little note to say—

Your heart's even bigger...

HAPPY
Valentine's
DAY!

Everybody's a Star!

My teacher directs our big school play
and *everyone* gets a part.
That's why it's *Snow White and the Fifteen
Dwarfs!*
(There were *seven* of them at the start.)

A Cure for the Crankies

I don't know how she does it.
My teacher can always tell
when I've got a case of the Crankies
(and the Grumpies and Grouchies as well).
She asks, "Is there something bothering you?"
and she listens to all that I say,
and when we're done talking, I suddenly feel
all those Crankies fly up and away.

Double Dutch

Who's that jumping in the middle?
Double-Dutch feet, watch them go . . .
Wait a minute—that's our teacher!
Who knew she's a jump-rope pro?!

Superhero Cleanup

My teacher can make even Cleanup Time fun.
At the end of each day there's a race.
We all play superheroes and go round to see
who can put the most things in their place.

Big BIG Dreams

"Dream big-big-BIG!" says my teacher.
"Do *anything* you want to do!"
So I ask, "Someday when I'm president,
will you still help me tie my shoe?"

See You Soon

It's our very last day of school today,
and we don't want to say, "Goodbye!"
'cause we know that our teacher will miss us
and we don't want to make her cry!
So instead we all say, "See you soon!"
'cause when we come back in the fall . . .

we'll all wave "Hello" to our teacher again
whenever we pass in the hall!